The KNOW-IT-ALLS
Mind the Store PETER LIPPMAN

Doubleday & Company, Inc., Garden City, New York

TO

MARCi
+
DOUg

Library of Congress Catalog Card Number 81-43432
Library of Congress Cataloging in Publication Data
Lippman, Peter J.   The Know-It-Alls mind the store.
   Summary: An inattentive but well-meaning alligator family minds cousin Angus's store in his absence, and chaos results.
   [1. Alligators—Fiction. 2. Humorous stories] I. Title. PZ7.L666Kn [E] 81-43432 AACR2
ISBN: 0-385-17399-7   Copyright © 1982 by Peter Lippman

Monday morning, Angus Know-It-All was all packed and ready to go on a trip when his cousins Father, Mother, Annie and Ernest Know-It-All arrived to mind his store.

Angus gave them lots of instructions, which he wrote on a blackboard so they wouldn't forget. The Know-It-Alls didn't listen to a word he said as it was all being written down.

Angus had barely left when the first customer entered the store. Father asked him what he wanted to buy. "A blackboard," he replied.

"Here's a real nice one. I'll just neaten it up for you," Mr. Know-It-All said as he wiped it clean.

Outside a man in a big car pulled up, honked and hollered to Annie, "Change the oil—I'm in a big hurry!" As Annie pulled the plug to drain the old oil, she called to Ernest to bring out a few new quarts.

"Sorry!" yelled Ernest.
"We just ran out of motor oil!"
"I'm certain we'll receive a delivery in the morning," Annie reassured the motorist.

The next customer to arrive ordered a soft ice cream cone. "Well that's simple enough," said Ernest, turning on the soft ice cream machine. He couldn't find the "off" button, so Annie filled a few buckets before Ernest realized he could just unplug the machine.

As the customer staggered out with his ice cream cone and two buckets of soft ice cream, another came in carrying a picture to be framed.

Father Know-It-All took it into the back,
and he measured and cut a piece of glass.
"Oops, that's a little too small," he said.
He tried again. And again. And again.
Soon there were no large pieces of
glass left.

Mother Know-It-All confidently solved the problem by cutting the picture in half and framing the pieces separately.

She then turned to a man who had come in for some green paint.

"I'm afraid we're all out of green paint," said Mother Know-It-All.

"Don't worry, I'll make some," called Ernest.

He took a can each of yellow and blue, poured them into a bucket, put them on the paint-mixing machine and, not reading the instructions, pressed the "start" button.

CAUTION—PUT
LID ON TIGHTLY
BEFORE STARTING
MACHINE!

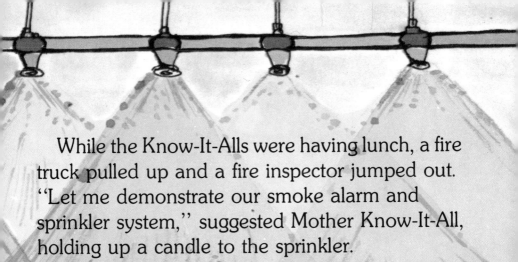

While the Know-It-Alls were having lunch, a fire truck pulled up and a fire inspector jumped out. "Let me demonstrate our smoke alarm and sprinkler system," suggested Mother Know-It-All, holding up a candle to the sprinkler.

After lunch, a little girl came in and picked out a toy airplane at the front counter. "No, no," said Father Know-It-All. "That one's for display. I'll get you a new one and show you how to fly it." Up the ladder climbed Father.

"Watch this one go," he said.
Unfortunately, he threw it a little too hard.
The plane went through the window and
Father Know-It-All landed in the
window display.

"It's just as well; I had been thinking we should sharpen up this window," said Father. "Why does Angus keep those pretty wool yarns all hidden away?"

As the Know-It-Alls closed the store
for the day and locked up tight,

DO NOT
TOUCH

they were pleased to see a crowd gathering to look at their window.

Bright and early the next morning Angus drove up with Francesca da Tutti-Sapienza, the great film director, on his handlebars. "I told you they could do it," Angus exclaimed.

"Eet ees wonderful, the perfect set for my great deesaster film!" Francesca cried.